"Her

Vivien Sparx

Email: viviensparx@hotmail.com

Facebook: www.facebook.com/vivien.sparx

Blog: http://viviensparx.blogspot.com.au/

Twitter: https://twitter.com/viviensparx

*If you cannot stop her in mid stride with
but a single glance...*
*If you cannot take her breath away with
but a single word...*
*If you cannot drop her to her knees with
but a single gesture...*
*If you cannot make her body quiver with
but a single touch...*

*Then all the toys and tools in the world will
do you no good.*
*Find her mind, grasp her heart and her
body and soul will surrender.*
-'shimmer'

One.

"Why are you punishing me like this?" Renee asked in a small, sweet voice.

Stefan smiled warmly. "It's not punishment. It's torture."

Stefan placed two squares of rich, dark chocolate between Renee's teeth and then glanced down to admire the slim curves of her body.

She was tied to the bed, her wrists and ankles fastened with silk scarves to the bedposts. Apart from a pair of white lace panties she was completely naked.

Stefan slid off the bed. He lit incense, and brought the glass of ice cubes and a candle into the room. He lit the candle and its warm flickering light cast a golden glow over Renee's body, highlighting the rise of her breasts and casting the flat hollow of her abdomen in darker shadow.

"There is a difference between punishment and torture," Stefan explained quietly. "Whips and beatings are not torture. They are merely a means to an end in some circumstances. Torture," Stefan continued in a whisper, "*is denial.*"

He saw the confused expression on Renee's face and he sat down on the bed beside her. Absently one of his hands rested lightly on the rising swell of her breasts. "Torture is denial," he said again. "It is denying yourself *that which you wish for most.* Understand?"

Renee shook her head.

"If I whip you, and command that you must not cry out – then resisting the urge to cry out is the torture. The whip is the means to the end. If I make love to you and deny you an orgasm, then denying yourself the release you crave becomes torturous. Making love to you is the method."

Renee furrowed her brow in concentration and thought about Stefan's explanation. Slowly she nodded and he saw the understanding in her eyes.

"Some Masters will whip their slaves in order to challenge them. Personally, I find that kind of brutality barbaric. But that doesn't mean the lesson of denial should not be taught, Renee. I simply have a better method."

The chocolate between her lips was warm and starting to soften. Her teeth sank into it and she felt her mouth fill with saliva. She hadn't had chocolate since moving in with Stefan. Now it was in her mouth... *and she couldn't eat it!*

"Now you understand," Stefan smiled. "I want you to keep the chocolate in your mouth, Renee, but under no circumstance are you permitted to eat it."

Renee nodded sadly. She could feel a thickness in her throat. Her tongue brushed the underside of the chocolate and the taste in her mouth was divine.

Stefan picked up the candle and let it hover uncertainly above Renee's body, moving it over her breasts, and then slowly down her abdomen. Renee's breath came in halting pants as she tried to anticipate the burn of the wax without opening her mouth any wider and swallowing the chocolate.

Stefan smiled. "No need to fear," he said. "It will burn a little, but it won't be painful. The ice on the other hand...."

Renee's eyes widened.

"This is my way of teaching you, Renee," Stefan explained. "Tonight I want you to understand the importance of denial. You must learn to control yourself at all times. You must develop the will to deny yourself *that which you crave for most* – whether it be to speak your mind without first obtaining my permission, whether it be orgasming without first asking for my consent... or any number of other challenges that will arise for you on a daily basis. Even eating chocolate. The ice and the melting wax are my way of teaching you this."

Stefan held the candle several inches above Renee's naked breasts. Her eyes widened a little.

Finally Stefan let a drip of wax fall near her left nipple.

Renee groaned. The heat was like an ant bite; a small sting followed by a lingering ache. Stefan watched the wax harden and the skin around the mark began to redden.

Quickly Stefan upended the candle again, dribbling a trail of hot melting wax down Renee's torso, all the way to the waistband of her panties. Renee sucked in a series of sharp breaths and felt tears welling in her eyes. She flinched at each new burn, writhing against the restraints, moving her body in a way that was not just a reaction against the sting of the wax, but also an unexpected erotic response. The drops of wax seared her like the sizzling touch of a lover's fingers; too hot to ignore – heating her whole body.

"Am I hurting you?" Stefan asked gently.

Renee shook her head. Now the sting of the wax had subsided, the warm lingering ache began to radiate. Renee could feel the muscles low in her abdomen beginning to clench with the slow pulse of rising arousal.

"Show me the chocolate."

Renee pouted her lips to show Stefan the chocolate that was beginning to melt in her mouth. The taste on her tongue was a constant tease.

"Very good," Stefan said. He lifted a piece of hardened wax off Renee's breast and studied the angry red mark it had left. There was a cube of ice in his free hand. It was melting. Stefan held the ice over the reddened skin and let the cold-water drip from his fingers.

The contrast between fire and ice was extreme. Renee flinched again and stifled a squeal.

Holding the ice, Stefan gently drizzled a wet trail over Renee's burning body, peeling away the spatters of wax as he went, and soothing her skin as if the ice were ointment. Renee's abdomen and hips began to slowly undulate as Stefan's gentle touch slid lower and lower and became increasingly sensual.

When he arrived at the lace of her panties he reached down and cupped her sex with his hand, feeling the dampness of molten heat that was pooling between her legs.

"You are aroused," he said.

Renee's expression was silently pleading. Her breathing sounded as a series of ragged little pants. She felt herself squirming against the pressure of Stefan's strong insistent fingers as they kneaded and caressed her through the thin silky fabric.

"Would you like me to do something about that?" he asked softly. "Would you like that, Renee?"

She nodded.

Gently Stefan leaned forward and plucked the melting chocolate from between Renee's lips. "You did well," he said holding up the squares up and inspecting the small teeth marks. "Are you starting to understand the importance of denying yourself that which you desire most?"

"Yes," Renee said softly. The taste of the chocolate was still on her lips and she licked them.

"Good," Stefan said. "Because denying yourself as a submissive sends a very significant message to your Master. It tells him that his needs are more important. It is a powerful way of showing your Master that you serve him – your denial is a symbol of your obedience."

"I understand," Renee said softly.

While Stefan spoke his hand between her legs continued to absently knead and tease, and Renee's attention quickly turned to the desire slowly uncoiling low and heavy in her abdomen.

Then Stefan popped the squares of chocolate into his own mouth and ate them slowly. He offered his fingers to Renee.

Renee sucked Stefan's fingers into her mouth, swirling her tongue hungrily and tasting the smeared chocolate. And then quickly her actions became more enthusiastic and wanton – as she did her best to intimate to her Master a much greater hunger than just a craving for chocolate.

As she sucked Stefan's fingers, so his other hand began to press more urgently through the damp fabric of her panties, encouraging Renee to re-double her efforts. Her tongue danced and fluttered over his fingers and her lips pulled him deeper into her mouth.

Then Renee felt one of the fingers on Stefan's other hand slide beneath her panties and press suddenly against the smooth soft pouting skin at her center.

She groaned and screwed her eyes tightly shut. Stefan's finger sank into her, and she felt the muscles in her legs tense and stiffen. Lying perfectly still – clenched and on the edge – Renee concentrated on the sensations that sparked like electric arcs along the length of her spine and flashed behind her eyes.

He was teasing her; she knew that. His finger was thick inside the molten heat of her and she wanted so much more, and yet she knew to ask was to admit the power he held over her. So she clenched her teeth and fisted her hands against the restraints as Stefan's finger teased her with exquisite skill; taking her to the brink and then backing away again and again.

"Denial takes determination," Stefan said.

Renee moaned softly and then suddenly arched her back off the bed as she felt a second finger ease inside her. She bit down on her lip to stop herself from crying out as her body clenched greedily. She felt herself grip and release as the heat at her core began to reach meltdown.

Stefan sensed it too. His eyes were locked on Renee's face, carefully watching her expression and gauging her reaction to his every touch. He knew he had her on the brink of an orgasm.

So he stopped.

The sudden feeling of emptiness was a shock to Renee and her eyes flew open in confusion. She gave a breathless, desolate groan.

He couldn't be serious! He couldn't leave her like this – not so close.

Not so desperately close!

"You are not permitted to orgasm," Stefan said. "I am sorry, but you have not done enough to earn such a reward."

Renee looked devastated. "Not done enough?" she pleaded. "What... what more can I do?"

Stefan's eyes were dark. "Deny yourself," he insisted. "Without complaint or question. You must reach the point where you instinctively accept my decisions...and only then will you have earned the right to orgasm."

Renee looked suddenly stricken. "How... how long will that take?" she asked softly. "How can I show you that I've already learned...?"

Stefan gave a tiny smile. "I don't know when you will be ready," he said. "But I will know. I'll know it by the way you act and by the way you accept all that I expect of you. It might take days... or maybe weeks of this kind of training before I am convinced you are deserving of release."

Renee shook her head in crushed disbelief. "You're not being fair!" she said, the words out of her mouth before she had time to realize her mistake.

Stefan's eyes turned flinty in an instant. He stared at her and his expression hardened to stone. "Fair?" he repeated softly, saying the word as though it was unfamiliar to him. "What does *fair* have to do with anything?"

Renee swallowed hard. There was a dangerous glint in Stefan's eyes – a menace that she instantly regretted provoking. She looked up at him bleakly. "I... I'm sorry. I didn't..."

Stefan shook his head. "No," he said. He made a cutting motion with his hand and Renee lapsed into silence. "You've said enough." He reached down to one of Renee's ankles and untied the restraint. Then he leaned across her body and untied the other. His face was grim. Now her legs were freed, he reached for the fabric of Renee's panties and tugged them roughly off her.

He stared at her – really stared – and there was a look on his face that she had never seen before. His eyes smoldered dark with the angry intensity of a slow-burning fire.

"You think you have learned denial?" Stefan asked. "You think you know what it is to be able to deny yourself that which you crave most?" He shook his head. "You think you have the willpower to reject what your body desires?" He was staring down at her and Renee didn't know what do. She wanted to cringe away from his anger, but she was still bound by her wrists. She wanted to apologize, but she knew it was much too late for that. Instinctively she started to draw her knees up to cover herself, but Stefan held her thigh and pushed her legs roughly apart again.

"You know nothing," Stefan said. "You know nothing about willpower. And I'll prove it to you." He put his hands between Renee's thighs and spread her legs wide.

"Deny yourself," he warned her. "If you cannot – if you orgasm – you will be punished in a way I know will cause you the most pain."

Renee closed her eyes and turned her head aside. She felt sick. Stefan's anger was like a slap across her face. She felt guilty. She had brought this upon herself for challenging him, and whilst Renee feared the threat of Stefan's punishment, an even greater fear was to be denied his approval.

He eased her legs wide open and Renee felt brutally vulnerable and exposed as Stefan's warm breath suddenly fluttered against her thighs. A delicious unbidden shiver ran through her. Then she felt the touch of his lips against the soft skin close to her center – and although his kisses were hungry and possessive, Renee felt herself melting and tensing at the same time.

She went wet in a rush. Her head rolled from side to side against the pillows. Her thighs flexed convulsively as Stefan's lips and tongue drew remorselessly closer, circling the swollen burning core of her and stroking her towards delirium.

His breath left her tingling – and then he took a long ravenous taste of her with the full width of his tongue.

A mewing cry escaped Renee's parted lips. She bit down as her breath hitched in her throat, and with a stifled gasp she arched her back off the bed.

Then Stefan pushed his tongue deep inside her.

A jolt went through Renee's body. The feel of his hard wet tongue devouring and savoring her was a sharp, sweet agony; a shock that hazed her mind and left her whimpering.

It was an overwhelming wicked delight, and Renee was powerless to fight him. Her head was spinning. She flexed her hands, desperate to cling to something, anything to keep her from crying out and begging for release.

Then Stefan gentled his mouth, lapping at the folds of her and swirling his tongue against her sensitized nub until the sensation was more than she could bare.

She clenched her teeth and tried to move her hips away for a second of respite but Stefan held her down with his hands, forcing her submission – forcing her to endure the exquisite intense primal ecstasy.

The intense power building low in her belly was like nothing Renee had ever experienced. It was like being on fire – every inch of her body ablaze. She twisted hard against Stefan's mouth and the heat within her spiked furnace-hot.

She tried to cry out – she tried to plead for release; knowing she would be punished but knowing also she could not resist the shimmering waves of fire and light that were beginning to spark behind her eyes. But the only sound she could make was a long, deep moan.

Her body was so tight and taut she felt on the verge of shattering apart. Her breathing came in ragged, short gasps. The tension was unbearable.

"Please..." Renee did not know what she was pleading for. All she knew was that Stefan's mouth and tongue were driving her to an erotic upheaval that was on the brink of spiraling out of control.

"Deny yourself!" Stefan hissed.

Her vision started to darken. "I can't!" she sobbed.

"You must."

"I can't. I....can't!"

Then it was too late.

Suddenly everything was incinerated in a blinding light so intense, so overwhelming, that it was almost painful. Renee felt her body reel and thrash, her legs kicking, her hips rising high off the bed. She felt her wrists painfully pulling against the silken bonds of her restraints. In an instant the oblivion of her orgasm consumed her.

Afterwards she lay on the bed dazed and shocked as her breath sawed in her lungs and her whole body shuddered through rippling tremors. She didn't want to come back from where she drifted because she knew all that awaited her was her shame and his disapproval – and the punishment for her body betraying her will.

"Shower and get dressed," Stefan's voice sounded hollow in her ears, cutting through the haze and forcing her back down to earth. She felt him tugging at the silk scarves around her wrists. "Meet me in the living room in thirty minutes."

Two.

"Defiance has consequences," Stefan said and his tone was as icy as an Arctic gale. "You disobeyed my instructions, and you disappointed me."

"I know. I'm sorry," Renee said, meaning it.

Since leaving the bedroom the edge had gone from Stefan's anger, but he had no intention of letting Renee know that.

"We had dinner plans this evening – your reward for three months of submission," Stefan began. "My first thought was to take that privilege away from you as a consequence, Renee."

She was standing in the middle of the living room floor with her legs spread, her hands behind her back and her head bowed, wearing just red panties and bra. But at the mention of the promised dinner Renee had so been looking forward to, she looked up at him sharply, horrified.

"Please..." she pleaded. "Not that."

Stefan's face was grim. "No," he said. "Not that. I will not deny you that reward for the effort you have made. The punishment should be directly as a result of your actions in the bedroom. But be warned – in the future, everything you earn as a reward can be taken from you for even a single moment of disobedience. Do you understand?"

"Yes," Renee said, her relief sounding in her voice. It didn't matter what her punishment was now, all that mattered was she was still going to dinner that night.

"Come here," Stefan pointed at his feet. "Position Two."

Renee knelt on the floor at Stefan's feet, spreading her knees on the soft carpet and then leaning forward until her cheek was resting on the ground. She clasped her hands behind her back and waited.

Stefan stepped behind her and got on one knee. He pulled her panties down until they were bunched between her spread thighs, revealing the taut cheeks of her bottom.

"Six," Stefan decided.

Renee closed her eyes and held her breath, feeling herself tense instinctively. She knew what was about to happen. Stefan stared down at her body, vulnerable and exposed, and was momentarily distracted by the perfectness of her figure. He traced a line down between her spread legs and gently rubbed the palm of his hand against her sex. Renee moaned softly as a rush of molten heat moistened Stefan's hand. She rocked her hips against his palm and he had to clamp down on the physical urge that lurched low in the pit of his stomach.

He pulled his hand away and then raised it high over her bottom.

"Never disobey me," he said – and landed the first slap hard on the fleshy part of Renee's right cheek. The sound was like a gunshot in Renee's ears, and the sting that came a split-second later made her flinch.

"That's one," Stefan said calmly. Renee's skin felt like it was on fire. Then he landed the second slap on the left cheek of her bottom. This one didn't seem to connect so perfectly. The sting was still intense, but she was prepared now. She bit her lip and kept her eyes screwed shut.

"That's two," Stefan said. He rubbed her bottom with gentle circling sweeps of his hand, taking the burn from his blows and seeming to spread it so that Renee felt heat down the backs of her thighs.

Stefan landed four more stinging blows, alternating between the inflamed reddened cheeks of Renee's bottom until the punishment had been completed. There was a mist of tears in Renee's eyes but she blinked them away.

"You can stand now," Stefan said.

Renee got to her feet and pulled her panties back up gently over her tender bottom.

"Do you have anything to say?"

"I'm sorry. Thank you for correcting my behavior," she said dutifully.

"You escaped lightly," Stefan said.

"I know."

"Don't disappoint me again."

"I won't," she said earnestly. "I promise."

Stefan sighed and glanced at the clock on the wall. "Very well," he said. "Our reservation at the restaurant is for 8pm. Go and get dressed."

Three.

Renee could not remember ever feeling quite so excited. She applied the finishing touches to her makeup and stepped back to inspect her reflection in the bathroom mirror.

In the three months since moving in with Stefan, this was the first time he had taken her out – and she had worked hard to earn the privilege. Her training as his submissive had been a relentless process; a lifestyle that she had taken to with enthusiasm and dedication.

She made a final turn in front of the mirror and sighed. It was the best she could do. She snatched her purse off the vanity just as she heard the clock in the living room begin to chime.

Renee appeared in the doorway dressed in dark blue silk, woven so finely that it seemed to float about her body with every movement, and as she stood there – waiting hopefully for his approval – the light from the bathroom struck through the sheer fabric, putting the long slender lines of her legs into silhouette. Stefan caught the shadowy shape made by the press of her firm pointed breasts beneath the plunging neckline and the faintest suggestion of her nipples.

Her hair was elegantly piled on top of her head; just a few stray curling tendrils wisping down past her ears, and her makeup had been so skillfully applied to emphasize the size of her eyes and the fine bone structure of her cheeks that it appeared as though she wore no cosmetics at all. She smiled, her teeth perfect and white against the lightly tanned skin of her face and across her bare shoulders and arms.

Stefan was waiting in the living room wearing a charcoal three-piece suit. His hands were behind his back and he turned, broad-shouldered and darkly handsome.

Renee stood nervously, and Stefan took a small, astonished step backwards as his breath hitched in his throat and he found it impossible not to stare.

"Stunning," he said, his voice almost hushed as his eyes drank in the graceful beauty of her. "You look like Cinderella."

Renee felt her heart flutter as she basked in the warm glow of her Master's approval. She stood a little taller and her face lit up in a delighted smile.

Stefan held out one hand to her and she came to him. "But there is something missing..." Stefan said slowly.

Renee's eyes widened. She looked down at herself in confusion. "I... I don't think..."

From behind his back, Stefan produced a small jewelry box and handed it to Renee.

"Do not get too excited," he said gently.

Renee accepted the box and lifted the lid. Set inside, on a layer of red satin, was a stunning diamond bracelet. Renee felt a rush of tears fill her eyes. Reverently she reached into the box and held the bracelet up. A small diamond and white-gold heart-shaped locket glittered and sparkled in the light.

"For me?" Renee asked in a whisper of disbelief.

"For tonight... and when you earn the privilege," Stefan nodded. He took the bracelet and fastened it around Renee's wrist. She shuddered deliciously.

"It is your conch," Stefan said.

Renee's brow indented in confusion. "My what?"

Stefan sighed. "Haven't you ever heard of William Golding?"

"No."

"Back in the 1950's an author by the name of William Golding wrote a novel called *'Lord of the Flies'*. It was a story about a group of British boys abandoned on an island. Didn't you learn this at school?"

She shook her head, mystified. This made no sense.

"In the story, the boys found a large shell, called a conch," Stefan continued. "They decided that whoever held the conch was the person who had the right to speak at their meetings. In other words, the conch became a symbol of democracy, and the right to voice their opinion. This bracelet is your conch."

Renee was still frowning. The significance of his gift was lost on her. Stefan took her hand in his and looked into her eyes.

"Whenever you wear this bracelet, Renee, you have the right to voice your opinion," he said patiently. "With this bracelet on, our relationship is not Master and submissive, it is man and woman. That means you can say what you think, and ask what you want without restriction."

The dawning realization of what Stefan was offering her suddenly set Renee's heart racing, and his words echoed like a love song in her ears.

"A relationship as man and woman..."

"And it's mine for tonight?" she asked tentatively.

"All night," Stefan agreed. "And for thirty minutes every day – unless you lose the privilege as punishment."

Impulsively, overcome by her excitement, Renee threw her arms around Stefan's neck and buried her head in his shoulder. "Thank you," she breathed. "You're the best Master in the world. I promise – I won't disappoint you ever again."

Four.

The *'Socrates'* was the finest restaurant in Bishop's Bridge – a converted street-side warehouse whose exposed timber beams and sandstone walls created a cozy, colonial atmosphere.

Stefan had arranged a limousine for the evening and as the vehicle turned onto Weaver Street, Stefan asked the driver to stop the car.

The restaurant was at the far end of the street. The driver opened the door and Stefan stepped onto the curb and held his hand out for Renee.

"It's a beautiful summer evening... and I want to show you off," he smiled.

They walked arm in arm to the restaurant, Stefan elegant and sophisticated, and Renee feeling as gangling and awkward as a schoolgirl beside him.

The doorman at the restaurant held the door open for them and Stefan nodded as the uniformed man smiled respectfully. Then they were inside, and the maître de led them to a candle-lit table in a secluded alcove away from other diners.

For Renee it was all like a fairytale; a dream more beautiful than she could ever imagine. She took a deep breath and closed her eyes for a moment, wanting to remember everything – wanting to burn the images into her mind forever.

"I imagine you have a lot of questions," Stefan said and then looked up at the waiter. He ordered a bottle of champagne.

"It's all so sudden," Renee gushed. "To be honest, I... I feel like I've been swept off my feet."

The habits of the last three months were hard to break, and she had to stop herself from looking down when she answered him.

"It may seem sudden," Stefan admitted, "But it is something I've been thinking about for some time."

"Really?"

Stefan nodded. "I just hadn't found the right moment."

Renee nodded thoughtfully. Then the waiter re-appeared. He filled their glasses with champagne and left the bottle in a bucket of ice beside the table. Renee waited until the waiter was gone before she spoke again.

"Can I ask you anything?"

"Yes."

"Anything at all?"

"Yes. Anything at all."

Renee nodded. "Then can you just tell me why?"

"Why what?"

"Why do this, Stefan? Why?"

Stefan picked up his champagne and studied the bubbles without drinking. He set the glass back down on the table and looked at Renee's puzzled expression in the flickering candlelight.

"The hardest, biggest question," he acknowledged. "I thought we'd start with small-talk first," he said wryly. Then he took a deep breath and leaned forward in his chair so their faces were close together.

"I want to let you into my life, Renee," he said. "I'm trying to include you. I know it may not seem much... but at the moment it is the best I can do. I know this may seem like a small step, but I'm trying to learn how to give up control, and to allow myself to begin enjoying being in a relationship again."

Five.

For Renee, dinner with Stefan passed in a dream-like haze. The food was delicious and she drank two glasses of champagne. She had never felt so happy. She had never felt so alive. She found the freedom of her bracelet liberating, and although reluctant to question Stefan on his past, it was more than enough that she was able to chat and laugh on equal terms with the dark gorgeous man who had her heart.

Most importantly, Renee sensed the first hints of intimacy in the way Stefan looked at her across the table and the way his hand touched hers whenever he made a point, or put forward an idea. When dinner was over and they left the restaurant, Renee felt like she was walking on air.

The limousine met them outside the *'Socrates'*, the driver waiting patiently beside the open door. Stefan asked the man to take the long way home and then he settled back in the plush leather upholstery. In the darkness he reached out and traced a finger gently down Renee's arm, making her skin prickle with goose bumps.

"A visitor is arriving tomorrow," Stefan said suddenly. "He will be staying in our home for the weekend."

Renee looked up at Stefan in surprise. "A friend of yours?" she asked hesitantly.

"No. Not exactly. He's an acquaintance from a long time ago," Stefan said, the tone of his voice oddly restrained. "He is a dom, and he is passing through Bishop's Bridge on his way to Washington.

He will be arriving tomorrow afternoon, and he will have his own slave with him."

"Is he a good dom?"

"He wasn't when I knew him."

"Why?"

"He was very strict — too strict for my tastes," Stefan intimated. "And he took too much pleasure in the punishment aspects."

Renee sat back thoughtfully for a moment. "What makes a good Master, Stefan? I mean, what are the qualities that are the difference between someone like you, and someone like this man you know?"

Stefan turned to Renee and studied her face. She was looking at him wide-eyed, genuinely curious. For an answer, he reached into his wallet and produced a small white card. He handed the card to Renee and she held it up to the light to read.

If you cannot stop her in mid stride with but a single glance...

If you cannot take her breath away with but a single word...

If you cannot drop her to her knees with but a single gesture...

If you cannot make her body quiver with but a single touch...

Then all the toys and tools in the world will do you no good.

Find her mind, grasp her heart and her body and soul will surrender.

-shimmer

"That was written by a submissive named *'shimmer',*" Stefan explained. "It sums up the differences better than I ever could. I keep the card as a reminder to myself about what every Master should aspire to."

"It's beautiful," Renee said softly, reading the words again. "No... it's more than beautiful.... it's perfect."

She handed the card back to Stefan, but he shook his head. "No, you keep it," he said.

They drove past the park and soon the limousine was slowing in front of Stefan's house. Renee stared out the window and waited for the driver to open her door. They were home, and Renee's thoughts turned once again to Stefan's guests who were arriving the next day.

Renee wasn't sure how to react. She felt vaguely jealous and resentful, and she realized it was because she didn't want anyone in their lives now this fragile new level of closeness between them had been reached. The night had been so perfect – Stefan had been so perfect – she resented the encroachment of anyone into the delicate cocoon of intimacy the evening had created.

"What must I do?" she asked. "How do you wish me to act around this man and his slave?"

"Just be yourself," Stefan said simply. "Remember your training and your place – especially around this man. And for the next couple of days you are to wear a short skirt and blouse, rather than just lingerie."

Renee nodded. She felt oddly disquieted. There was a brooding sense of melancholy around Stefan and it seemed to infect her own mood. "I'll be on my best behavior," she said. "I promise I won't disappoint you."

Six.

The sullen atmosphere lingered around Stefan until they were in the bedroom. Then, as if in an effort to forcibly brush off his heavy mood, he grabbed Renee's hand and pulled her toward him.

Renee did not resist. She was willing to be used in this way; eager for him to use her body as a salve for his gloom.

Stefan reached to comb his fingers through her hair, carefully removing the pins. Renee felt the faint tugs against her scalp. Her eyes were locked on Stefan's and she felt a sudden delicious tingle of excitement when she saw the familiar glittering darkness move behind his eyes.

Stefan's mouth came down on hers with determination and hunger, and Renee sensed a rush of heat low in her abdomen. She felt the forceful slide of his hands tangling in her hair, felt his fingers wrap themselves around the nape of her neck as he held her head to allow himself full access to her mouth. The kiss went on and on, until Renee felt her whole world spinning with the aching throb of her own growing need and desperation.

Finally Stefan pulled his lips from hers. The blaze of lust in his eyes was unmistakable.

"Kiss me back," he urged her in a hoarse whisper.

Renee threw her arms around his neck, pressing the heat of her body into his, molding herself against the muscles of his chest. Wantonly she ground her pelvis hard against him and a wild reckless thrill of exhilaration fizzled inside her. She kissed him fiercely, trying with that kiss to show the physical need that raged within her. Her tongue flicked tentatively, and then more frantically, exploring the edges of Stefan's mouth. A new unknown power surged through her; the power to take and to arouse – the power to initiate and to demand.

Stefan's hands went down to the narrowness of her waist as he held her to him. He couldn't seem to get enough of her. Her sweet honeyed taste was intoxicating. The fit of her mouth against his, the tiny murmurs she made in the back of her throat that told him her need was as strong as his. She kissed him back with such a passionate recklessness that Stefan felt the clench of his fiery need, making him hard and ready.

His mouth slid from Renee's lips and he trailed hot kisses down her neck. She threw her head back and there was a low sexy growl in her throat. Stefan's mouth slid lower, across her shoulders as his hands slid up her arched back, deftly peeling away the silken layers of her dress.

The wispy fabric fell away from her breasts and Stefan sucked one of her hardened nipples into his mouth. His hand cupped the warm flesh of her breast and Renee felt the insistent tugging send tiny electric jolts of arousal to every tensed and trembling part of her body. She wrapped her hand around the back of his head, fisting her hands in his hair.

"Oh, yes," she moaned, as he suckled and nibbled at her. "More, Stefan. Please...!"

Her hand slid down between them and brushed against the weighty hardness of him, her fingers fluttering and uncertain, but becoming bolder as he moaned his encouragement. She flattened her palm against him, rubbing her hand up and down, feeling the swollen shape of him and thrilling in the way he pulsed beneath her fingers.

"Take them off," Stefan said.

A shock wave of raw need surged through her, and then Renee's fingers were tugging at the buckle of his belt and trembling as she dragged down his zipper.

At last she had his trousers undone and she took him in the warmth of her hand, her fingers splayed and stretched to hold him.

Stefan pulled his mouth from her breast. There was a simmering heat in his eyes. He tugged at her dress and it bunched at her hips. He tugged again and it fell in a silken pool around her feet.

Stefan kicked off his shoes and socks and then he took a pace back to admire the beauty of Renee's body. She stood before him in just tiny red panties, and her whole body seemed as tense and arched as a bow by the depth of her arousal.

Her training told her to stand and let him drink in the sight of her as he tugged off his tie and loosened the buttons of his shirt. But she remembered the bracelet, and she was already drunk with the heady power of her new freedom. Bravely she dropped to her knees and wrapped her arms around his waist, pulling Stefan towards her open mouth.

To have him standing before her – to have the power over his pleasure in the way she used her mouth – was a new experience for Renee and she reveled in the freedom as she teased and tasted

Stefan's hardness. Each kiss and swipe of her tongue brought a deep groan from Stefan, and she drew out his aching need until her taunting simply became too much for him.

He reached down and grabbed at her arms, loosening her grip around his thighs. He pulled her to her feet and then pushed her hungrily onto the bed. Renee fell backwards onto the soft mattress and her legs fell open in silent invitation.

Then she felt his naked body over hers. He was so hard, so masculine, his muscular legs like iron. She could feel him pressed between her thighs, hard and huge as he cupped her beasts in his hands. He suckled one nipple, then the other, teasing with sweeps of his tongue until she gasped with agonized pleasure.

There was no time to peel her damp panties off; their need was too urgent. Stefan merely hooked a finger in the waistband and snapped the thin elastic, tearing the lingerie from her. Then, with a groan, he entered her. The fullness of him slid deeply inside her and Renee undulated her hips and then wrapped her legs around his waist.

"Yes!" Stefan moaned. He raised himself up on his braced arms and drove into her with powerful thrusts that she met with fierce lunges of her own.

He was her man and she belonged to him for all eternity. The words echoed in her mind like a mantra in time with the rhythm of their bodies as Stefan filled her again and again. Then, on the edge of their explosive releases, he covered her gasping mouth with his, so that the instant of their orgasms was shared in a wild kiss that left them breathless and heaving in exhaustion.

Afterwards, slick and sweaty from their lovemaking, they showered together. Stefan watched Renee as she tilted her head back beneath the cascading water. The sight of her slim, perfect body arched and glistening wet as the water sluiced over her breasts and hardened nipples was an irresistible taunt. Under hooded eyelids she flicked him a teasing glance and Stefan took up the invitation in her eyes with a growl. He pushed her against the cool glass partition of the shower and made love to her against the wall as hot water covered them, and the hissing spray drowned out their strangled cries of passion.

Seven.

Renee drove into Bishop's Bridge the next
morning for groceries. When she returned home it
was late afternoon. Stefan was standing in the
living room, staring out of the curtained window.
His jacket was thrown over the back of a chair and
his shirtsleeves were rolled up to his forearms.
There was a tumbler of scotch in his hand. Renee
sensed instantly the brooding tension in his stance;
the stiffness in his shoulders and the stillness of
him.

She went silently into the bedroom and hung her
clothes neatly in the wardrobe, pulling on a short
black pleated skirt over her panties and a white
tank-top over her bra.

Her collar was on the bedside table and as she
picked it up her fingers brushed over the diamond
bracelet Stefan had given her.

The conch.

She longed to be able to slip the bracelet on right
now! She wanted to know what it was about the
man who was arriving that darkened Stefan's mood
so completely.

With an effort, Renee set her fears aside. She
turned to the mirror and checked her reflection.
She brushed her hair quickly and re-touched her
makeup. She sighed. Strangely, she felt restricted
in the skirt and top, even though the hem of the
skirt barely covered her upper thighs and the fabric
of the tank stretched across her breasts like a
second skin.

She fastened the collar around her throat and closed the bedroom door behind her.

When she came quietly back into the living room, Stefan seemed to sense her presence. He turned, his face bleak. His eyes flicked over her almost absently. Renee waited with her legs spread, her hands behind her back and her head bowed.

"Fine," he said at last. "Those clothes will be what I expect you to wear for the next couple of days."

Renee nodded. She waited for Stefan to say something more but he simply turned back to the window.

"I have groceries in the kitchen. May I attend to them?" Renee asked after a long moment of awkward waiting.

"No," Stefan said suddenly, and she saw the tautness in his face and the deep lines of tension that framed his mouth as he turned to her. "Master Larry has just arrived."

Eight.

Larry Madden slid out behind the wheel of the slick silver Porsche and stretched. He was a tall man with big arms. He was wearing jeans and a shirt, the top four buttons undone revealing a swollen chest covered with ginger hair and a belly that looked flat and hard.

He squinted up at the afternoon sun and then turned to face the house. Renee noticed the thickness of the man's neck under a wide flat-featured face with dark beady eyes. He ran his hands through his short wiry hair and yawned expansively.

"Stand in position," Stefan said to Renee and she obediently went back to the center of the living room and spread her legs. She clasped her hands behind her back and took one last look at Stefan as he went out through the front door before she quickly bowed her head and waited...

She heard Stefan and Larry talking on the doorstep and Renee was struck by the volume of the man. His voice boomed, the sound of his words grating and gravel-like. She heard the man laugh at something Stefan said, and then he was filling the doorway, standing with his hands on his hips, and Renee felt her skin creeping with the force of his eyes on her body.

"Ruck me!" Larry Madden said, and whistled softly under his breath. He came into the room and slowly circled Renee – and it took all of her will and discipline not to cringe away from his leering inspection.

"Master Larry, this is my slave, Renee."

Renee lifted her head and stared at the man. He reminded her of a snake; there was something vulgar and reptilian about his manner, but she kept her expression blank and her voice neutral. "Pleased to meet you, sir," she said.

"And it's a rucking pleasure to meet you," Larry bared his teeth. He turned back to Stefan in the doorway and punched his shoulder lightly. "You've done well for yourself," he said. "What's it like? What's the ride like?"

"Renee has been with me for three months," Stefan said stiffly. "And she is a very competent submissive."

Larry stopped and stared at Stefan, noting the strain in his voice. He tilted his head curiously. "What?" he challenged. "Am I too crude for your little bit of fluff, Stefan? Is that it?"

Stefan said nothing. The two men stared at each other and the tension between them was like electricity. Then Larry slowly began to smile.

"Well, it's got nice tits, I'll say that much for you. Are they real?"

Without waiting for an answer he threw himself down on the sofa and stretched out. "We were always the smart ones, you and me, Stefan. We always knew how to pick a good slave, didn't we, eh? Yes we did. You and me should be friends after all we went through together in the old days."

"Of course we're friends," Stefan said solemnly without a trace of sarcasm in his voice. "I consider you one of my best."

"Yeah?" Larry asked, his face suddenly earnest. "Go figure! Jesus, I always thought you looked down your nose at me," Larry said, shaking his head in wonder. There was the smell of stale sweat and alcohol on him. "Even after what I did for you – I always thought you didn't like me."

Stefan gave a faint smile but said nothing more. He turned to Renee instead. "Please go out to the car and help Master Larry's slave, Renee."

With a silent sigh of relief, Renee went down the stairs and was met by a slim blonde girl who looked almost child-like. She had big sad eyes and a serious expression. She was wearing a skirt shorter than Renee's, high heels, and a lacy bra. Renee was struck by the size of the young girl's breasts; they seemed enormous in proportion to the thin athletic frame of her body.

The girl smiled weakly at Renee and then lowered her eyes again without saying a word. She had a scuffed and dirty travel bag slung over her shoulder and a suitcase hung heavy from her other hand. Renee took the suitcase and led her inside the house.

Renee put the suitcase in the hallway as the young blonde girl followed her inside.

She eased the travel bag off her shoulder and stood in position beside the bar.

Larry waved his hand at the girl. "Get me a beer," he said.

The girl bent over the travel bag obediently and reached inside. "Not a warm one this time," he instructed.

The girl reached around inside the bag for a moment and found a bottle of beer. She unscrewed the cap and brought it to where Larry sprawled on the sofa.

He took the bottle without even glancing at the girl and held the beer to his lips, drinking slowly. When he set the bottle down again it was half empty. He looked at Stefan. "Want a beer, friend?" Larry asked – and then he belched loudly.

Stefan raised his eyebrow but said nothing. He slid his hands into the pockets of his trousers. Only Renee noticed that her Master's hands were bunched tightly into fists.

"No?" Larry said, looking hurt. Then he smiled lazily and his hand snatched out and locked around the blonde girl's wrist. His grip squeezed like a vice. She didn't move. She didn't flinch.

"Well how about some of this?" he laughed. Using his weight, Larry pulled the girl down to him and tipped her backwards over his lap. He pinned her down with one heavy muscled arm across her chest and with the other hand he swept her tiny skirt up over her waist.

"Take a look. She's all yours if you want a ride, Stefan."

The girl was naked under the skirt, her lower body shaved completely smooth. Larry drifted one of his big hands across the girl's sex and she squirmed.

"You can even go first," Larry offered. "That's what buddies do for each other. That's how friendships work."

Stefan glanced down at the girl. Larry's hand had forced her legs apart and now she was lying exposed and docile.

"No. Thank you," Stefan said. "But I will have a drink with you," he smiled thinly. He went behind the bar and poured himself a scotch.

"To the future," Stefan said. He raised his glass.

Larry looked at him suspiciously. "To the past," Larry said. "Where friendships were formed."

The two men drank in silence, and Stefan watched Larry carefully over the rim of his glass.

"What's her name, Larry?" Stefan waved his empty glass at the young girl. "Where did you get her? She's very pretty."

Larry's eyes narrowed for a moment warily, and then lit up at the compliment. He pushed the girl off his lap and she stood at his side with her head bowed.

"I call it Tink," Larry said. His beer bottle was empty and he studied the label for a moment in contemplation before he went on. "Bought her brand new from our contact about two years ago." He winked.

Stefan inclined his head. "You've done well."

Larry smiled. "She cost me six grand," he said. "And she was a bitch to train. Had to do it the hard way for the first few months – but she got the message."

"How old is she?"

"Eighteen."

Stefan smiled. "That's young. But if I remember, you always did have a thing for the young ones."

Larry laughed and rubbed his chin. "Don't you talk bucko!" he laughed loudly. "If I remember, you got your rucking scar because of a new piece of fluff."

Stefan smiled but it never reached his eyes.

Larry got up off the sofa and belched again. Then he casually pulled the strap of the girl's bra down revealing her large firm breasts. Larry pinched the girl's nipple but her face remained completely expressionless.

"These cost me another three," Larry boasted. "Had to get 'em done in Mexico because of her age, but, man, they're the bomb! What do you reckon, Stefan? Aren't they amazing?"

Stefan feigned admiration. He watched Larry absently caressing the girl's swollen breasts and then he turned to Renee. "Take Tink into the spare bedroom please, Renee," Stefan said. "You can help her to unpack the suitcase while Master Larry and I do some reminiscing about the old days."

Renee skirted around the edge of the room, subconsciously putting space between herself and Larry. Dutifully, the young blonde girl followed her into the hallway and retrieved the heavy suitcase.

Larry watched the two women disappear as he crossed to the travel bag and rummaged around inside for another beer.

Nine.

Renee pushed the spare bedroom door open and stepped aside as Tink came into the room behind her, struggling under the heavy weight of the suitcase. With a grunt, she hefted it onto the bed and sprung the latches.

Renee smiled at the younger girl. "My name's Renee," she said. "What's yours?"

"Tink," the girl said.

"I mean your real name."

The girl frowned. "Tink."

"Don't you have another name? Like Christine or Claire..."

"Not that I remember."

As they spoke, Renee watched the girl unpacking the bag, dividing the contents into two separate piles. One bundle was a collection of dress-shirts, new denim jeans, a business suit, sports jacket and several pairs of leather shoes. The second pile was made up of just two lacy bras, two pairs of black lace panties, and a simple blue sundress. Beside the clothes the girl set a tiny cosmetics bag.

"Oooh," Renee pretended. "I love the color of your dress. Can I see it?"

Carefully the girl handed Renee the dress and she unfolded it and held it up in front of her. It was short, ice-blue in color, and Renee could see areas where the fabric was almost threadbare. Under the left arm, she noticed a tear in the material had been hand-sewn.

"Master bought it for me from a thrift shop when he took me from Arizona," Tink said shyly.

Renee smiled and ran her eye over the meager collection of clothes Tink had packed. "Well... I don't know how you do it," she said kindly. "I could never travel so lightly."

Tink frowned and tilted her head in a question. "Lightly?"

"Yes. I need three suitcases just to stay overnight."

Tink looked down at the floor. "This... this is everything I own," she said.

Renee slid the empty suitcase under the bed and sat on the edge of the mattress while Tink began to hang her Master's clothes neatly in the wardrobe.

"I heard your Master say you had been with him for two years," Renee began. "You must have been interested in the lifestyle at a young age."

Tink said nothing. She put all the shirts onto coat hangers and then lined up all of her Master's shoes in pairs.

"What made you want to become a submissive and serve a Master?" Renee persisted.

"I didn't have a choice," Tink said, but there was no emotion in her voice – no bitterness or longing. "I was trained – and then sold."

"What about... what about before you were trained?" Renee persisted, even though she could tell the girl resented being questioned.

"I don't remember," she said. She put her panties, bra and cosmetics case in the bottom draw of a bedside table. "I don't remember anything before I woke up in a cage in Arizona and a man told me I had been brought to him for training as a sex slave."

Ten.

"I can't believe you and that man were once friends."

Stefan shook his head. "We weren't."

Renee pulled the covers down and sat on the edge of the bed. "Well he certainly thinks you were."

"Larry Madden is – and has always been – a drunken thug."

Renee watched as Stefan undressed and climbed naked into bed. She looked at him, a concerned expression creasing her brow. "Well clearly you have a history together."

"Ancient history," Stefan muttered.

Renee unfastened the cord around her bathrobe, peeled it off her shoulders, and climbed under the covers. She lay on her side and watched Stefan's face. "He said you got a scar or something. What did he mean? Is that how you are connected to this man?"

Stefan closed his eyes for a moment and when he opened them again he was grim-faced.

"I met Larry Madden shortly after my wife died," he explained. "Renee, at the time I was angry. I was mad at God for taking Tif from me – and I was mad at the world. I had just discovered the world of BDSM and I wanted to know more. There is a dark side to domination and submission, and I accidentally got drawn into it."

"A dark side?"

"Dark and dangerous," Stefan said solemnly. "Renee, girls like Tink are bought by men like

Larry. There is an underground business, and it's big money people-trafficking."

Renee propped herself up on her elbow and looked hard at Stefan. "What do you mean?"

Stefan sighed. "There is a man in Arizona," he began, "and he is well known in the BDSM world. He's a supplier. He goes by the name of Victor. Young women are kidnapped and brought to him for training. That's what he does. They call him 'The Animal Trainer'. He takes these girls and he breaks them down, and then re-makes them as sex slaves. Then they're auctioned off to the highest bidder."

Renee shook her head. She was horrified. "You're not serious."

"I am," Stefan said. "These girls – girls just like Tink and even younger – are taken and trained to serve their Masters. And men like Larry buy them. The younger and the prettier they are, the higher the price they eventually fetch."

Renee sat in silent shock for long moments. "I can't believe people like that exist," she said slowly. "I can't believe things like that happen."

"They do," Stefan assured her. "I told you once before, Renee, that beyond the romance there is reality – and sometimes that reality can be harsh and horrible."

"And you were involved in this.... this crime?"

"No." Stefan said emphatically. "At the time I didn't even know the Arizona auction block existed. I simply met Larry at a BDSM club and we got to talking. He invited me to Arizona. I went with him. Then, in a bar a day before the auction, I got into a fight with a scumbag who was treating a woman badly. The guy pulled a knife.... and during the fight I got stabbed. Larry was drunk. As I reeled away bleeding, Larry fell onto the guy's blade and got stabbed too."

Renee listened in stunned silence, shaking her head as Stefan re-told the story. Tentatively, she reached out and ran her finger down Stefan's muscular chest. "You've got so many scars," she said. "You look like an old tomcat. Which one was the knife?"

Stefan took her hand and guided it to a raised white scar on the right side of his abdomen. She gently ran her finger over the ridge.

"And Master Larry? You said he got stabbed too."

"Yes," Stefan said. "Unfortunately. He got stabbed in the chest. And ever since that day he's figured that I owed him."

"Because he got stabbed instead of you."

"Yes — even though it wasn't how it happened."

For a long time Renee lay beside Stefan in silence.

Finally Stefan rolled onto his side to face her. "You're shocked."

"Yes, of course," Renee admitted.

"So was I when I first found out about Victor and the Arizona auctions," Stefan said.

Renee shuddered. "Were you.... were you ever like Master Larry is? Were you ever so mean to your submissives?"

Stefan shook his head. He held her eyes and his expression was sincere. "Never. Not once," he said. "I've changed a lot since I first became involved in BDSM, Renee, but I never started from the same evil place Larry did. I was never that cruel. I was never that kind of man. Larry hasn't changed – he's the same brutal bastard he was when I met him."

Renee reached for his hand and clutched it tightly. "I spoke to Tink when we were unpacking," she said. "She's scared of him, Stefan. She didn't say a lot, but she didn't need to. I could tell by what she wouldn't say that he was cruel."

Stefan nodded. "I wouldn't have expected anything different," he sighed. "But it's none of my business, Renee. Or yours. What Larry does with Tink is up to him. Once he leaves here he's out of our lives for good – and as far as I'm concerned any 'debt' between us will be paid."

"I think Tink was kidnapped," Renee said sadly. "When we talked today, she said she can't remember her life before she arrived at that place in Arizona, Stefan. She would have been about sixteen! Somehow, her entire life before then has been erased from her memory."

Stefan nodded. He had no doubt the 'connection' Larry Madden had referred to earlier was Victor and that Tink was one of the girls who had endured his 'Arizona School'.

Renee squeezed Stefan's hand tightly and shuddered. "I'm so lucky," she said softly. "Lucky I have you as a Master and not someone like him."

Stefan smiled and hugged her close to him. "No," he said. "Renee, I'm the lucky one. I've changed so much because of you. It's like I'm waking up again after being asleep for so many years. I feel like the old me is coming back to life; the man I was before I became immersed in this world. I have you to thank for that." He kissed her tenderly – a long lingering kiss that was more about the emotional than the physical. When at last he eased his mouth from hers, Renee sighed dreamily and rolled onto her back. "You took my breath away," she said softly.

Eleven.

The next morning Stefan reluctantly took Larry downstairs and showed him the punishment room.

Hands on hips, Larry whistled as he stood in the center of the low-ceilinged room and looked around. "Jesus!" he said. "You've surprised the hell out of me, bucko."

Standing back in the doorway, Stefan watched as Larry went around the room, touching the pieces of equipment and occasionally crouching to inspect the leather harnesses, ropes and chains. On one wall hung a collection of whips. Larry picked up a leather riding crop and tested the flex between his hands. He swished the crop and it cut through the air.

"I thought you were a softie," Larry grinned. "I never knew you were such a kinky bastard. It's always the quiet ones you gotta look out for."

Stefan kept his face impassive. He stared at Larry. "It's what I did for a living," he reminded the big man. "Clients came to me to learn about submission. It made sense to introduce them to some of the typical equipment they might encounter."

Larry gave an exaggerated nod and scratched the back of his head with the handle of the crop.

"That's right," he said. "Now I remember. Stefan's seedy school of submission or something, isn't it?"

Stefan didn't smile.

Larry hung the riding crop back on its hook. There was a low wooden trestle in the far corner of the room. It looked like a builder's saw horse. The timber frame of the structure had been fitted with leather padding and leather cuff restraints. Larry took a moment to admire the craftsmanship of the piece, and then leaned nonchalantly against it.

"Well, you know what they say," he said slowly. "Those that can't do.... teach."

Stefan bridled. Everything about Larry Madden was a challenge; a taunt. He was a big man and accustomed to getting his own way. He was crude and confronting. He was used to intimidating people – menacing and threatening them until they cowered and buckled. But Stefan was a big man too, and there was a limit to his courtesy. Without realizing it, Larry was fast approaching that limit.

"They say that..." Stefan agreed off-handedly. "At least the dumb ignorant ones do."

There was a long tense silence, and then Larry Madden threw back his head and laughed. "A comedian!" Larry chuckled. "That's what you are. A bloody comedian." His laughter turned into a fit of coughing, and by the time he had regained his breath he was watery eyed... and the tension between the men had eased as Larry's expression suddenly became mischievous.

Renee and Tink were standing in position with their heads bowed and their hands behind their backs just inside the doorway. Both women were wearing short skirts. Renee wore a pale yellow tank-top, whilst Tink was wearing the same bra she had worn when she arrived the afternoon before.

Larry's eyes drifted over the two submissives and he leered at Stefan. He rubbed his chin ruefully.

"Mind if I try some of this fancy equipment out?"

Stefan stiffened. He glanced in Tink's direction. "I suppose not."

Larry smiled. "Mind if I give your bit of fluff a test drive? You know – just for a comparison?"

Stefan smiled, but it was ice-cold and dangerous. "When hell freezes over."

"My, my, my…" Larry put his hand on his hip and lifted one eyebrow in a pantomime of arrogant surprise. "No need to get so defensive, bucko." Larry thought he should be offended by Stefan's refusal. "She's precious is she? She got something special under that little skirt has she?"

Without taking his eyes off Larry, Stefan snapped his fingers and Renee looked up. "Go upstairs, Renee," he said calmly. "Wait for me in our bedroom."

Renee stepped past him and went up the stairs quickly. When she was out of earshot, Stefan said with suppressed anger, "You get one chance with me, Larry. And that was it. Understand?"

Larry held up his hands in mock surrender and took a step backwards. "Woooah, the sheriff in these here parts don't like anyone messin' with his livestock, eh? Okay, bucko. No offence, okay?" his tone became conciliatory. He stepped over to Tink and grabbed her wrist. He dragged her over to the edge of a sturdy wooden bench, bent her over, and then he lifted the girl's skirt to make sure Stefan could see she was naked underneath. Larry retrieved the riding crop from the wall and turned back to Stefan in invitation.

"Want to join me?" Larry offered. "She likes the whip, she does. Likes it a lot. Best damn way to warm her goodies up. Give her a few cuts with the crop and you'll see what I mean."

Stefan could see the fearful expression on Tink's face. The young girl looked terrified.

"But she's done nothing wrong," Stefan pointed out calmly. "Why would you punish her?"

"Because I can!" Larry snapped. "Because I feel like it. Because it makes me happy. Treat 'em mean and keep 'em keen."

Stefan shook his head. "Larry, why don't you give the girl a break. Wait till she deserves to be punished."

"Why don't you give me a break?" Larry growled. "I don't tell you how to treat your fluff – so why don't you get off my back!" He pushed Tink's legs wide apart and then the crop hissed in the air as Larry flicked his wrist. A reddened mark appeared on the back of the girl's thigh. She flinched and then whimpered.

Larry turned. He was smiling. He held the riding crop out to Stefan in invitation. "Last chance..."

"No. Thanks," Stefan said. "I've got my own submissive to train – and it's not how I do things." He turned to go, and then paused. "Don't hurt the girl, Larry. I'm warning you. Don't you dare cross that line."

"You're soft!" shouted Larry. "That's your bloody problem. You don't have what it takes. You never bloody did. Jesus wept. What's happened to you, man? You're not acting like no dom. You're acting like you love the bitch!"

Stefan closed the door behind him and stood alone at the foot of the staircase. Words, he thought. Just words... but Larry's bitter taunt had cut through Stefan's protective armor and as he slowly climbed the stairs, he wondered whether maybe Larry was right.

Twelve.

When Stefan entered the bedroom he found Renee pulling clothes from her wardrobe and tossing them over her shoulder onto the bed. It looked like she was packing. She was grim-faced and there were angry furrowed lines across her brow.

Stefan leaned against the doorway and folded his arms, watching her silently as she muttered to herself.

She saw him from the corner of her eye. "He's a brute," Renee said as she tossed a yellow blouse onto the growing pile of clothing.

Stefan said nothing. He noticed Renee had slipped the bracelet onto her wrist.

"He shows her no kindness — no compassion," Renee said. "He doesn't treat her as a submissive. He treats her like .... like..." she couldn't find the word she wanted and she stomped her foot in frustration.

"Like a possession?"

"Worse!" Renee reeled around. "Much worse." There were angry red spots of color on her cheeks.

Stefan came into the bedroom and closed the door quietly behind him. "It's not our business," he said. "Larry can do what he wants with Tink, and Tink can leave him if she's unhappy."

Renee laughed hollowly. "Can she, Stefan? Can she really? And where would she go? He *bought* her, for God's sake."

Stefan nodded. "You're right," he admitted. "But there is a fine line here, Renee — and I won't interfere unless Larry crosses it. I don't like the way he treats the girl any more than you do... but I won't get involved unless I am sure he's abusing her."

"But you will get involved if he goes too far?"

"In an instant. You have my word."

Renee looked into Stefan's eyes. She believed him. She trusted him completely.

"Thank you," she said, mollified enough to calm down a little. She took a deep shuddering breath and he hugged her.

"Now, please tell me what you are doing?" Stefan changed the subject. "Why are you throwing clothes around the room?"

Renee glanced at the pile of clothes on the bed. "I am cleaning out my wardrobe," she said. "When I helped Tink unpack their suitcase last night she told me she only owned one dress. I was going through my wardrobe to see what clothes didn't fit me anymore. I was going to offer them to her."

Stefan smiled. Renee's generosity didn't surprise him. "Good idea," he said.

"I can't stop him treating her the way he does. But I can show her some kindness."

"You're a sweet person. And you have a good heart," he said. He looked at the bundle of clothes and didn't recognize any of the garments Renee had selected. "So when is the fashion parade?"

In an instant the atmosphere subtly altered. A warm wave of feminine understanding washed over Renee. She looked up into his face and there was a smoky, sultry hint of arousal in the way she moistened her lips before she spoke. "Right now – if you would like to watch."

Renee turned for the bed but Stefan followed her.

"Wait."

She stopped obediently and he came up behind her. She felt the touch of his hands on her waist and she shivered deliciously as he lifted her tank-top. She raised her arms in the air as he undressed her. Then his fingers were at the zip of her skirt. It fell to the ground around her ankles. She waited passively as he slipped the straps of her bra off the smooth soft skin of her shoulders and unfastened the catch.

"Now," he said softly.

She crossed to the bed in just her panties, as light on her feet as a dancer, each step now a gentle emphasized sway of her hips; a subtle provocation for him.

Stefan was sitting, elegant and masculine, in the wing-backed leather chair across the room. His eyes were dark and hungry, but there was more than raw lust in the attitude and language of his body.

He was appreciating her.

She was parading herself for his pleasure.

She was his prize, and she felt proud to be so. He thought she was beautiful, and she felt honored to be his woman. He judged her desirable, and she felt intoxicated by the knowledge.

Renee felt the familiar liquid heat of her own arousal clench low in her abdomen as her blood began to quicken.

She reached across the bed for an emerald green dress, coming up on her toes to flex and tense the lithe muscles of her legs, and then she pirouetted to face him.

"Drop the dress," Stefan said.

She did.

He stared at her, slim and young and achingly beautiful; his woman – his submissive.

Stefan came up out the chair, hunting towards her, his hands unfastening the buttons of his shirt as he closed the space between them. Renee felt her breath hitch in her throat and her heart began to race with exhilaration and anticipation. He was all man, and she belonged to him.

Without consciously realizing it she lowered herself to her knees in the attitude of submission and as he entwined his long fingers into her hair she drew down the fastening of his trousers and instinctively opened her mouth to pleasure him.

Stefan threw back his head as exquisite sensations overwhelmed him. "Yes!" he hissed. And then a moment later, "faster."

Renee felt Stefan's hands move to her shoulders, and his touch was gentle and then suddenly firm. She felt his fingers clawing into her and she knew it was a measure of the passion he felt. He pulled her to her feet and wordlessly unfastened the diamond bracelet from her wrist.

Renee understood instantly, her body so attuned to the rhythm of his that she responded instinctively to every gesture and every nuance of his manner.

She acquiesced to his unspoken message with a submissive bow of her head, giving her body to him – understanding that the fuel for his desire was a raw need to take her.

Stefan let the bracelet fall to the floor, and scooped Renee up into his arms. He carried her to the bed like a conquering warrior bearing a mighty prize, and stood over her as she laid waiting at his mercy.

Renee closed her eyes and felt the firm demand of Stefan's hands roaming over her body, melting her like wax, peeling off her dampened panties, and then strumming his fingers across the soft moist lips of her sex.

"Please..." her voice was strangled and agonized with the intensity of her arousal.

Stefan undressed quickly. Renee felt the weight of him and the warmth of his body beside her. She threw her arms around his neck.

"Oh, God, you're so hard and strong," Renee gasped, her voice tremulous. "Oh, sweet God I need you."

He bent to kiss her and Renee's lips parted beneath the demanding pressure of his. Far from resisting, she kissed him back, matching his passion, her desperation just as powerful.

Fluid and strong he came over her, sliding between her thighs, feeling her body trembling with her own pent-up desire. She was impatient for that first thrust, anticipating the delicious feeling of being stretched around him and the press of his pelvis hard against her own.

Stefan pushed himself deep inside her and they both went still, staring at each other.

She was hot, and wet. And tight.

Renee's inner muscles clenched around him and she groaned with an uninhibited sensuality. He shifted his weight slightly, sinking further into her, a careful erotic movement of his hips so that their bodies seemed to fuse.

Stefan's eyes were dark. His senses reeled. He pressed his forehead to hers as he fought the urge to pound himself into her. He laid perfectly still, his teeth gritted against the powerful waves of lust, calling up every ounce of his iron self-discipline and willpower.

Then Renee whimpered... and the small passionate sound seemed to slip the leash on all of Stefan's tightly restrained hunger.

The muscles in his chest and biceps tensed as he plunged deep. The feel of her body molded to his drove him forward. He filled her again and again. He heard Renee gasp, and felt her hitch her knees higher, begging him for more with her body.

Renee's heart pounded crazily. Another helpless whimper sounded deep in her throat. Her breasts were crushed against Stefan's chest, their dusky pink nipples tightening and tingling. The breath gushed out of her and she sucked in another. She could feel every pulsing inch of him and it drove her to raptures.

There would be other times for them to share the slow lingering delights of gentle lovemaking, but now his need was too sharp, too urgent to be denied. And Renee's own burning hunger was ignited by the hardness of him. She cried out again – a fierce sound filled with joyous relief – burying her face in the taut muscles of his chest as he filled her completely and she sensed the last inhibitions of his restraint slip away.

"Yes!" she encouraged him. "Take me. Use me, Master. I want all of you. All of you."

Stefan growled his hunger; the sound as primal as the instinct. The breath drummed from his chest. Renee arched underneath him as he thrust into her and his fingers hooked cruelly into her flesh.

"Yes!" she hissed again.

No longer able to be passive to his need, Renee ground her pelvis against Stefan, writhing her body in erotic undulations that drew him deeper into her and locked their bodies together. She was desperate for more. She needed more.

The heat was too intense.

Stefan's need was too fierce to be contained.

His release came with a mighty surge; an explosive combustion of energy that tore a ragged groan from his mouth and filled his vision with flashes of blinding light. Renee clung to him, and an instant later she felt her breath seize in her lungs as her body clenched and pulsed, sweeping her away on the same surging wave of blissful euphoria.

Thirteen.

With her arms full of clothes, Renee used the instep of her foot to tap at the bedroom door. A moment later Tink cracked the door open and frowned at her.

"C'mon! Open up," Renee said brightly. "Before I drop everything."

Still wary, Tink held the door open and Renee made a light-hearted display of staggering under the weight of everything she carried. She tossed the clothes onto the bed and then sagged onto the edge of the mattress.

"What are you doing?" Tink asked quietly, her arms folded defensively.

"Cleaning out some things I don't wear anymore," Renee said. "I thought you might like to look through these dresses and tops to see if there's anything you liked."

Tink's expression became bewildered. She stared wide-eyed at Renee, uncertain, distrusting; wary and unsure.

"I... I... can't..." she started and then stopped. Her eyes were drawn to the inviting pile of fabrics on the bed. There were more clothes here than she had ever seen in her life; glittering gowns, beautiful shimmering silks. She took a hesitant step towards the bed and then stopped again.

"I... I can choose anything?" she asked, not really believing it.

"You can have them all if they fit," Renee smiled. "You would be doing me a favor. They all have to go... I'd rather they go to someone who might like them."

"All?" Tink's eyes filled with tears. "All of them.... for me...?"

"If you want them."

She reached out for the clothes, and then pulled her hand back as if it all might be a trap. She stared at Renee and Renee smiled warmly. "Please," she said. "Have a look through them."

Tink went to the bed in a dreamlike daze, and brushed her hand over a turquoise blue blouse. She felt the silk fabric between her fingers and she shuddered.

"Try it on!" Renee smiled. "That color would be perfect for you."

Tink bit her lip. For one last moment she resisted... and then the lure of such a luxury simply overwhelmed her and she set aside the last traces of her suspicion. She picked up the blouse and hugged it to her cheek, marveling at the cool soft feel against her skin.

"It might be a bit tight around the chest," Renee said. "You're bigger in the bust than I am."

Tink slid her arm into the sleeve and Renee came around behind her to help. She pulled Tink's hair free from the collar and then scooted around in front of her to start on the buttons. Tink was crying.

"I'm sorry," she sniffled. "I... I'm just overwhelmed."

Impulsively Renee hugged the girl and heard her inhale sharply and stiffen within her embrace.

Renee dropped her arms and took a small pace back. "Sorry," she said. "I guess you don't like hugs."

Tink's bottom lip was trembling and she gave Renee a brave little lop-sided smile. "I've never had one before," she said softly.

So Renee hugged her again.

With the buttons on the blouse fastened, Tink ran her fingers over herself, caressing the fabric. The length was perfect, and although it was a little tight around the bust, it felt heavenly against her skin.

Urged on by Renee she self-consciously twirled around and there was a girlish giggle in her throat and a uniquely feminine expression on her face as she waited for Renee's opinion.

"Stunning!" Renee clapped her hands. "It's perfect on you."

Suddenly Tink was weeping. Smiling at Renee gratefully and weeping. She did not sob – the tears simply welled up from underneath her enormous eyes, broke from the lashes, and rolled gently down her cheeks.

And still she smiled.

"Thank you," she said.

"You're welcome," Renee grinned. "Now…. let's see if we can find a matching skirt!"

The two women lost themselves in another hour of dressing up as Tink tried on skirts and more blouses. Some of the pieces did not fit, but even then there was the simple pleasure of each other's company as Tink's shyness melted away like a morning mist and she smiled more freely and giggled more often.

Tink's collection of new clothes grew steadily until they had tried on every piece. She sat back on the bed, her eyes glittering delightedly as she surveyed the most precious collection of treasures she had ever known in her life.

"Thank you again," she said and her hand tentatively sought out Renee's.

"You're welcome, again," Renee beamed, glowing with the knowledge that — for the moment at least — Tink had known that someone in the world cared.

"Oh, wow!" she said suddenly. "Let me go and see if I can find some shoes for you!"

*

Larry Madden came into the bedroom with an ugly scowl on his face — his mood dark as thunder.

There was a beer bottle in his hand. He saw Tink, and his eyes narrowed to mean little slits. The girl, attuned to her Master's tempers, backed away from him, sensing danger.

"What have you been up to?" Larry snarled. "I've been calling you! I needed another ruckin' beer."

Tink bobbed her head, eager to please. "I'm sorry," she said. "I was with Master Stefan's slave. She... she gave me some clothes."

Tink pointed to the clothes she had carefully folded — and Larry's eyes misted over with sudden violent rage.

"Clothes?" he spat. "You don't need ruckin' clothes!" He threw the beer bottle at the opposite wall, and Tink cowered away from him, seeking safety in the corner.

Larry stalked to the bed and grabbed the first piece of clothing within reach. It was a turquoise blue women's shirt. He bunched it up between his clenched fists and ripped the garment to pieces.

Horrified, Tink took half a pace forward, a shocked, anguished pain in her face.

"No!" she cried... and then realized her mistake.

Larry turned on her, his eyes wide, his brows arched, and his face a mask of absolute horrified disbelief.

"What did you say?" he asked, and his voice was barely a whisper, laced with dreadful menace.

Tink backed away. She was distraught and crying. Larry picked up another piece of clothing. It was a green dress. He held it up threateningly. "I asked you what you said..." he repeated.

"No." Tink said in a small voice.

"That's what I thought you said," Larry's lips curled up into a satanic sneer. He tore the dress to pieces, and then threw them onto the ground. Tink watched in horror – and then Larry's hand lashed out and snatched her by the wrist.

"You will not defy me!" he roared. "You will not. By God, I'll beat that out of you right now!"

He was a big man, and she was a slim child-woman. She was no match for him. With one hand locked around her throat, and the other pinning her arm painfully behind her back, he marched Tink along the hallway... and then down the dark gloomy stairs towards the punishment room.

Fourteen.

"Master! *Stefan!*" Renee's face was twisted with her horror. "He's doing it again!" Her eyes were filled with tears of outrage and frustration. "He's got her downstairs in the punishment room, and he's beating her this time, Stefan. He's beating her!" Her hands were clenched into tight angry fists.

Stefan dropped the book on the ground and lunged from the reading chair, getting to his feet in a single swift move that was filled with suppressed rage.

He took Renee by the shoulders and held her at arm's length.

"Are you sure, Renee? Are you certain it's not just punishment?"

"I'm sure," Renee sobbed. "Stefan she's crying. She's begging. He must have her tied or chained. And he's beating her repeatedly."

"How do you know this? What were you doing downstairs?"

"I was in our bedroom getting some shoes for Tink," Renee said. "I thought I heard my name called. I thought it was you. I started down the stairs — and then I realized what was happening," she said. *"Stefan, I think I'm the cause of this! I think he's angry about the clothes I gave her."*

"Okay," Stefan's face went as hard as granite. "Come with me."

Stefan went down the stairs in a rush, with Renee two steps behind him. At the bottom of the stairs he didn't stop; he simply used his momentum and threw his shoulder against the door of the punishment room. The door flew open, smashing backwards against its hinges and Stefan burst into the room.

Tink was bent over the wooden saw-horse, with her wrists and ankles tied. Larry was standing over her, his shirt open, his body glistening with sweat and his breathing ragged from exertion. In his hand was a short leather riding crop. He froze in the act of raising the whip as Stefan's broad-shouldered bulk filled the doorway.

Stefan looked past him to the girl. She was naked, and her back was criss-crossed with dozens of angry red welts. She was sobbing uncontrollably, her tiny frame heaving, racked with pain.

"What do you want?" Larry's eyes blazed. "Get the ruck out of here!"

Stefan bunched his fists and took two steps towards Larry.

'The fact that you are this girl's Master does not mean you can ever forget you are a man – and no man does this to a woman. This isn't discipline or punishment. It's abuse – and it's cowardly." Stefan kept his voice low and steady. He held Larry's eyes for long seconds, and then Larry looked down and lowered the riding crop.

"I don't like bullies, Larry. And you're a bully. You always were," Stefan said. "I think it's time you were taught a lesson."

Larry laughed but it came out hollow. He hesitated, wiped his lips nervously with the back of his hand.

"Is this how you treat the man who saved your life?" he looked hurt. "Stefan, Jesus, she's just a slave."

"She's a *woman!*" Stefan hissed.

Larry's eyes darted around the room. He was looking for an escape that wasn't there. He threw the crop down and bunched his fist. "You like to think you're the big dangerous man, Stefan," he growled. "But I'm dangerous too. I'm dangerous in ways you can't imagine."

Stefan smiled. He drifted closer to Larry until the two men were standing toe to toe. They were a good match. Larry was a big strong man, and he had an inch of height on Stefan. But Stefan had momentum... and a burning rage.

"I'm going to hurt you," Stefan said. "Not as much as I should. Not as much as you hurt this girl. But enough that you will remember it." His face was set and pale, his dark eyes merciless, but despite that he kept his voice quiet, making the threat all the more menacing.

Larry started to smile... and at the same instant Stefan launched a right handed upper-cut that caught the big man flush on the jaw. Thrown from the level of his waist, the punch had all of Stefan's weight and anger behind it. The impact sent Larry reeling backwards. His arms cartwheeled for a handhold and then his legs went from under him. He fell heavily to the ground.

Stefan went up onto the balls of his feet, his fists bunched and cocked like hammers. "Get up, you filthy coward."

Larry stayed on his back. He opened his mouth wide and moved his jaw from side to side. The pain was huge and his ears were ringing. Gently he felt the side of his face. Already the skin was swelling into an ugly red lump.

"Get up," Stefan growled again.

Larry groaned – and then laughed, but there was something very wrong with the sound of it. Stefan knew then that Larry wasn't going to fight.

"You are out of my house in the morning," Stefan said. "And don't ever come back."

Fifteen.

"I can cancel this meeting if you would feel better?"

"Yes," Renee said. "Please cancel it. I'm scared."

Stefan turned sharply. "Of Larry?"

Renee frowned at him. "No. Of this woman you're going to meet. I'm scared you are going to fall in love with her."

"Be serious for a moment. Do you want me to cancel?"

"It depends," Renee said. "Is she pretty?"

Stefan sighed. "Renee..."

She held up her hands in surrender. "Stefan, go to dinner. Master Larry is semi-conscious. In fact I don't know how he hasn't passed out yet with all the beer he's drunk."

Stefan frowned. "You should have let me kick him out this afternoon."

"We couldn't. He'd kill someone driving in his condition. At least if he sleeps it off tonight he'll be sober in the morning."

Stefan turned back to the mirror and Renee's thoughts turned back to the real cause of her concern.

"You're a man of the world," Renee sat mournfully on the edge of the bed. "You can probably tell if a woman is pretty just by the sound of her voice, right?"

Stefan rolled his eyes. "We're not back on this again are we?"

"I think I have a genuine concern!" Renee pouted. "I don't want to lose you to another woman."

He turned to her. "You're being silly."

Renee sighed. She climbed off the bed gloomy-faced and stood close in front of Stefan. He was struggling with his tie, and with Renee now blocking his view he had to lean around her to see his reflection in the mirror.

"Let me," she said. She undid the tie and re-tied it, adjusting the knot until it sat neat and flat against the buttoned collar of his shirt. Stefan watched her as she worked, her face a beautiful child-like picture of concentration. Finally she put her hands gently against his chest. "Done," she said.

Stefan leaned to the side to inspect her efforts.

"Hey," he said lightly. "That's pretty good."

Renee went back to the bed and threw herself down onto the mattress. "Why can't I come with you?"

"Because it's a business meeting."

"Tell me again why this woman called you. What does she want to talk about — and why does it have to be at a restaurant?" She was jealous and she didn't mind that Stefan knew it.

Stefan sighed. "Renee, she is a journalist. She wants background about the BDSM lifestyle. Now, you put that bracelet on ten minutes ago. Do you really want to spend our time going over this? Isn't there something else you would rather talk about?"

"You mean Master Larry, and how he treats Tink?"

"No. Not that either. But how is she... and where is he?"

Renee's brow furrowed. "Tink is resting in their room," Renee shrugged. "We had a brief talk, but I don't know what she will do. I told her she could stay here for a while if she wanted – but I still think she'll go with him. It's the only life she knows."

Stefan nodded. He wasn't surprised. "And where is Larry?"

"On the sofa, still drinking," Renee said. "I saw him when I came out of the bathroom. With any luck he'll sleep through the night – if he's not asleep already."

Stefan grunted.

Renee rolled onto her side to watch Stefan as he tugged on his jacket. Her eyes roamed over him appreciatively, admiring, as she always did, his muscled broad-shouldered physique.

She was wearing a bath-robe and her hair was still wet from her shower. She deliberately tugged the robe apart so the material gaped to expose her long brown legs. Stefan caught a glimpse of her reflected in the mirror and he turned to admire her.

When she knew he was watching, Renee closed her eyes and rolled onto her back, spreading her legs and pulling at the cord that cinched around her waist. The robe fell wide open and Renee began to lightly caress herself, her fingers like feathers as they skimmed across her breasts and down the hollow of her abdomen.

Stefan came closer to the bed, watching her hungrily. He felt his arousal clench sudden and urgent like a fist.

"I'm very, very horny..." Renee announced in a sultry breath. She stole a peek at Stefan and recognized the lusty expression on his face as he stared down at her.

"I just want to...to...." and then she groaned as her hand glided down and gently cupped the heat between her parted legs.

Stefan watched mesmerized as Renee's fingers began to massage and tease her sex. He was entranced, his eyes darting from the blissful expression on her face to the way her hand circled and moved with growing urgency.

His own arousal sparked by Renee's overtly sexual display, it was only the faint chime of the living room clock that suddenly broke the spell. Stefan blinked, then recoiled away from the bed, a knowing smile on his face.

"Cunning," Stefan conceded, "but not clever enough. I've got to go." He checked his watch.

Renee sat up, the suggestive temptation of her performance forgotten in an instant, her face now even more dejected.

"It's six o'clock. I should be home before nine," Stefan said. He leaned over the bed and kissed Renee on the forehead. She made one last futile attempt, clutching shamelessly for his crotch, but he skipped out of her range like a boxer and headed out the door towards the garage.

Sixteen.

Larry Madden heard the car reverse out of the garage and then accelerate away into the night.

"Stefan bloody big-shot," he snarled, his voice a little loud and his words a little slurred from the alcohol. "Mister high and bloody mighty!"

The bottle in his hand was empty. He dropped it onto the sofa beside him.

"Tink!" he shouted. "Get out here, you lazy bitch!" he roared. "I want another beer, y'hear me?"

The girl came from her room, her footsteps light and nervous. She went to the kitchen and brought a beer to Larry, cold from the refrigerator. She approached him like a gazelle approaching a water-hole; her senses heightened, fearful and on edge. Larry snatched the beer from her hand, spilling some of its content over himself.

"Ruck me!" he shouted. He looked at Tink's small pale face and saw the terror in her eyes as he raised his hand to strike her.

Tink cringed, and closed her eyes... but the blow never came. "Get out of my sight," Larry hissed drunkenly at the girl.

No. It wasn't her. Tink wasn't the one he was angry at. It was Stefan bloody wonderful he was angry at. Stefan the cock-sure bastard. Stefan – *the bastard who owed Larry his goddamned life!* Stefan and his bloody precious bloody slut. Him and her. Him... and her....

Him.... and her....

Larry looked around the empty living room with narrow malicious eyes. Then he chuckled and licked his lips with the quick-darting tip of his tongue.

"I think it's time for the bloody big hero to learn a lesson about loyalty," Larry muttered. "Reckon he needs to know you always gotta pay your debts."

He hauled himself up off the sofa and ran his hands through his hair. His head felt itchy. He scratched at a lump on his neck and looked around the room.

"Tink!" he shouted suddenly.

The girl re-appeared in the hallway, standing meekly out of his reach. He crooked his finger and she took tiny reluctant paces towards him.

"Listen to me," Larry grabbed her around her throat. "You go to the room and you stay there. Close the door. You hear me? You stay there until I come for you," he shook her threateningly. "Don't matter what you hear — you stay in that room till I fetch you."

Tink nodded and backed away. Larry watched her all the way until she went back into the bedroom and pushed the door closed behind her.

Larry bared his teeth. He fingered the swollen lump on his jaw where Stefan had knocked him down, and suddenly his mood turned vengeful and ugly. "Time mister bloody wonderful learned how dangerous I can be," he said grimly, "and time I collected my payment."

Seventeen.

Renee stepped into the en suite and regarded her reflection with honest appraising eyes. Was she pretty? Should she really be worried about Stefan falling in love with another woman?

She leaned closer to the mirror, turned her head slightly to one side, and pulled a pouting face. She ran a finger down her cheek; her skin felt soft and flawlessly smooth – but still she wondered...

Her bathrobe was still open and she looked at her body's reflection dispassionately. Were her breasts still firm? Was she putting on a little weight perhaps? Maybe she needed to exercise more.

She reached for the hairdryer and turned it on. Her hairbrushes were in the top drawer of the vanity. She pulled open the drawer and found a comb. And when she straightened and looked in the mirror again, Larry Madden was standing behind her.

Renee yelped in fright and dropped the dryer. It smashed on the tiled floor.

"What are you doing in my bedroom?" she demanded. She whirled to face Larry and backed away from him until she felt the edge of the basin against her legs. Her heart was racing, and her hands trembled as she tugged the bathrobe tight around her and fumbled with the corded belt.

Larry chuckled softly. He licked his lips and there was a dangerous look in his eyes. "I've come to collect from your boyfriend," he said. "And you are the payment."

Renee's eyes widened. "No!"

"Yes!" Larry rasped forcefully, his anger and excitement making his breathing ragged. His hands were clenched into fists at his side. "I think it's a fair price, especially since the way I've been teased."

"Teased?" Renee gasped. "I haven't –" she shook her head.

"The way Stefan's been protecting you ain't natural," Larry shook his head slowly. "It ain't right. You're a piece of fluff. That's all... so why ain't he willing to give me a turn on you? What's it matter to him, eh?"

As he spoke Larry very slowly closed the space between them. "Something wrong with me is there?" he asked. "It don't make sense. I would have given him a ride on Tink... so what is it about you that's so special?"

Renee kept her widening gaze on him as she edged away. She could smell his fetid breath and she cringed towards the corner of the room.

"You must be special for sure," Larry grinned. "You must have something red hot. Reckon I'm gonna find out. See what all the fuss is about."

He reached out for her and she swiped his hand away. He laughed. "I'm in no hurry," he leered. "We've got time." He rubbed his chin, the sound of his stubble crackling like static. His hand snapped out again, this time cobra-quick, and his fingers hooked into the knotted belt around her waist. He tugged and the loosely tied knot unraveled. Renee's robe fell open and his eyes narrowed hungrily.

Renee's breasts were everything he had imagined; full-sized and firm, with beautiful budded nipples. She gasped and tried to cover herself. Larry slapped her arm so hard that she felt the limb go numb from her elbow to her wrist.

Renee doubled over in pain and Larry lunged for her.

One hand went round her waist and the other smothered her mouth as he spun her off balance. "Make a noise.... any noise at all... and I will snap your neck." He spoke hoarsely into her ear. The smell of his breath was warm and sour in her face. "Just stay still and pretend I'm Stefan." And he chuckled.

Renee felt the hand around her midriff moving as he pushed her robe aside. Then she felt the hot clammy touch of his hand on the naked flesh of her hip, sliding quickly downwards, and the horrific jolt of it shocked her into desperate struggles.

Larry kept chuckling, holding Renee easily as her legs kicked and flailed and her body twisted against his grip. He lifted her off her feet and crushed his arm tight around her waist, driving the air from her lungs. "Don't make me do this the hard way," he hissed.

Renee felt a wave of sudden nausea overwhelm her and tiny pinwheels of light flashed behind her eyes. Then she was being hauled backwards out of the en suite.

Larry threw Renee onto the bed. She tumbled awkwardly. Her robe fell wide open but she didn't notice. She felt the back of her head crack against the headboard of the bed, and then saw Larry's big body hunting towards her. She opened her mouth to scream and as she did Madden clenched his fist and hit her in the face.

The warm coppery taste of blood filled Renee's mouth as Madden crawled onto the bed. He clamped a hand around her throat and squeezed, pinning her helplessly. Renee's hands scratched and clawed at his arm, gouging out tiny wounds. He ignored them

"Not a sound," Madden growled. He used his free hand to fumble for the zipper on his jeans.

Suddenly there was a scream behind him and Madden turned to see Tink standing in the bedroom doorway. She had a kitchen knife in her hand.

"Get back in the room, Tink!" Madden roared at the girl. "Do it! Right now, or I will beat you until you can't stand up."

"Let her go!" Tink cried.

Madden laughed at her. Tink edged closer. The knife wavered in her shaking hand. "I said let her go!"

He watched her come closer.

"Get back in the room!" Madden hissed, "or you'll be next!"

Tink lunged at Madden with the knife, stabbing at the broad of his back. Madden waited until the girl was close enough, then he twisted and caught her by the wrist with his free hand. He squeezed. The knife fell from Tink's nerveless grip and she fell to her knees beside the bed moaning in pain. Madden rolled onto his side and kicked the girl in the face. She fell backwards and didn't move.

"Now we can be alone," Madden licked his lips. He released his grip around Renee's throat and she gulped in painful lungsful of air. Madden bunched his fist and punched her in the face again.

Renee went still. She felt the fight ooze from her body as roiling waves of darkness threatened to overwhelm her. She felt her arms falling loose by her side. She felt rough hands tugging her legs apart. Her vision blurred as she felt Madden's weight crushing down on her.

His flat, ugly features filled her vision. He was grunting. She could feel the putrid smell of stale beer on his breath as it gusted over her face. Sweat dripped off his brow into her hair and trickled down her cheeks.

But there was no pain. No pain at all. Just the feel of his body crushing down on her and a sense of helpless revulsion as he continued to fumble between her legs.

She thought it ended quickly, but she wasn't sure whether she had passed out and it had gone on and on. She heard him growl in her ear; a raw sound of strangled frustration.

She blinked her eyes and realized he was standing beside the bed. With the weight of him off her she felt like she might be floating.

Her vision swam out of focus for a second and then cleared again. Madden was fumbling with his clothing, staring down at her with a dull, remote expression on his face. He dragged the back of his hand across his mouth and she saw he was trembling.

"I should have known you wouldn't be worth it," he said.

He slapped her hard across the face and finally – blissfully – the darkness of unconsciousness overwhelmed her.

Eighteen.

Stefan knew instantly that something was wrong.

"Renee!"

He came through the side door at a run, stalking through the house. His heart was racing. His blood pounded loud in his ears. "Renee! Where are you?"

He burst into the bedroom and felt the strength go from his legs so that he had to clutch desperately for the doorframe.

Renee was lying on the bed. There was blood on her chin and spattered across the pillows. Her robe was open — her naked body spread out — her legs bent awkwardly and tangled in the bed sheets. Beside the bed lay the crumpled body of Tink. She was slumped half-sitting against the bedroom wall.

"Jesus!" Stefan hissed. "Sweet Jesus, no."

He walked slowly to the bed. He felt cold and numb.

Please, God. I beg you. Not again! Please let her be alive. Please don't take her away from me — I couldn't live with the pain of losing her too.

"Renee," he said softly. "Renee." He knelt beside her and touched her face. There were ugly purple bruises around her throat and the side of her face was swollen and grazed. Her skin felt cold. He wrenched his hand away and felt icy dread cramp in his stomach.

Renee's eyes fluttered and he sobbed his relief. He ran his eye quickly down her body and then back to her face. He saw her take a shallow breath and an enormous rush of emotion washed over him.

"Oh, thank God," the words choked in his throat. "Thank God!"

He went to her, pulling her close to him, his touch gentle and achingly tender. He could feel the soft even beat of her heart against his chest.

He held her for a long time, rocking her gently. Gradually, as if waking reluctantly from a dream, Renee stirred and looked up at him through hollow, vacant eyes.

"It's okay," he whispered. "You're okay." He was crying. For the first time in years, Stefan was crying. He brushed a stray strand of damp hair from her face as she lay quietly in his arms. Then he stooped to kiss her, his lips lightly brushing over hers. "I love you, Renee," he whispered hoarsely.

He felt such an eternity of affection for her then – as he had never felt for any other person – and he was astounded by the strength of it.

She opened her mouth to speak, but no words came. He touched her lip softly with his finger. "I know," he said. "You don't have to say it."

Suddenly, from the corner of his eye Stefan saw a flicker of movement and he turned his head to see Tink. Her eyes were dull and dazed and she was feeling the back of her head and wincing.

"Are you alright?" Stefan called to her. The girl used the wall to get slowly to her feet. She nodded and then winced again.

"What happened?" Stefan asked.

"Larry."

"Did...? Did he...?"

"No."

"Are you sure?" Stefan had to know.

Tink nodded slowly. "He kicked me in the face and I fell against the wall. Then... then he tried...to....but he couldn't get it up. He couldn't get himself hard," she said. "He was too drunk."

Stefan's relief lasted just a moment, and then, as he held Renee in his arms, it became something darker. Something terrible and black as the rage began to burn in him.

He clenched his jaw and closed his eyes, letting the anger come, letting it fill him until it blazed through his body like a forest fire.

Stefan touched the livid swelling around Renee's throat. "I have to get her to a hospital," he said at last. "Do you need a doctor?"

Tink shook her head. She tottered unsteadily to the bed.

"Why not call an ambulance?"

Stefan shook his head. "It will be faster if I drive."

He picked Renee up in his arms, cradling her close to him. Tink pulled her robe tight around her body. "I'll help you get her to the car," she said.

"Grab a blanket," Stefan nodded back at the bed. "She's in shock. I need to keep her warm."

Tink draped one of the blankets over Stefan's shoulder. "Wrap it around her when she's in the car."

The sensation of movement roused Renee and she came alert. She struggled feebly and tried to speak again. Stefan lowered his face close to hers. "I'm okay," she said softly and licked dry lips. "I want you to go after him."

Stefan shook his head. "No," he said. "You are all that matters to me. I've only loved two women in my life," he said softly. "The first I lost, and I was helpless to do anything. I won't lose you."

Nineteen.

It was a fifteen minute drive from the estate where they lived through to Bishop's Bridge, and then a further ten minutes to the local hospital.

Stefan drove carefully on the narrow winding roads, accelerating at every opportunity along the straightened sections of carriageway and then taking the treacherous corners with elaborate care as they leaped out of the darkness. His eyes constantly diverted from the darkened view through the windscreen to Renee who sat quietly beside him.

She was huddled in the blanket, slumped in the corner, her face ghostly pale in the reflected lights from the car's dashboard.

Her breathing was shallow and steady, but Stefan could see the labored pain in her expression each time she exhaled through her damaged throat.

He pulled the car to the side of the road and flicked on the overhead cabin light.

"Are you okay?" Stefan asked gently, taking a moment to tuck the blanket tightly around her.

She turned her face to him, and he was grateful for that at least; she could hear him and she was alert. But it was her eyes that shocked Stefan the most. They seemed to have expanded to an enormous size, and under each was a darkening bruise-like smear. The pupils of her eyes were enlarged and dulled, lacking the intelligent glitter he was so accustomed to.

"I'm alright," she said. Her voice was a reedy, rasping whisper and she winced and tried to swallow. Her cheeks were streaked with tear tracks, and the swelling around her jaw made her face seem distorted. He reached underneath the blanket and when his hand found hers he squeezed.

Stefan got the car back on the road, and stabbed his foot on the accelerator. A long tree-lined straight section of tarmac stretched before him. He flicked the car's headlights onto high-beam and heard the engine under the bonnet growl.

Then suddenly red tail-lights appeared on the road ahead. Stefan cursed under his breath and came down through the gears.

As he drew closer, he frowned. The car ahead wasn't where the road was...

He stomped on the brakes, bleeding off speed quickly, and then realized the vehicle had gone off the road.

The road to Bishop's Bridge cut through dense woodland, winding its way along the contours of the hills that surrounded the town. The driver of the car had lost control and smashed through a guardrail, crashing head-on into the barrel-like trunk of a redwood tree.

Under the glare of headlights, Stefan saw a man standing in the middle of the road. He was waving his arms.

It was Larry Madden.

The rage returned to Stefan, boiling up, fizzing in his blood. For a moment his foot hovered over the accelerator – and then he slammed on the brakes, tyres squealing as he slewed the car to a halt in a billowing cloud of blue smoke.

In the corner of his eye he saw Renee stir. He turned and realized she was staring at him.

"I'm going to finish this," he said.

"I want you to," she nodded.

Stefan got out of the car and walked purposefully towards Larry. Backlit by the car's headlights, Madden didn't realize it was Stefan until the last moment – until it was too late.

The shock registered on Madden's face, and then Stefan was on him.

Stefan's first punch was a wild, rage-filled blow that landed on the side of Madden's head. The big man went sideways, falling to the ground. Dazed, and unable to flee, he rolled away from Stefan and scrambled to his feet.

Madden backed away like a trapped animal, until he was cornered against the wreckage of the Porsche. On the ground beside him he saw a broken tree-branch the length of a baseball bat. He bent down and picked it up.

"Come on, then!" Madden growled. "I'm gonna tear you apart!"

He took a pace forward, lifting the branch like a club - and as he did, he realized he had made a mistake. Stefan wasn't retreating away from the threat. His hands were low and his fists were bunched. His lips were drawn back tightly, baring his teeth. His eyes were black, and there was a furious satanic expression on his face.

Madden realized Stefan was coming for him and the shock of it slowed him. He couldn't bring the branch down before Stefan closed the distance. Stefan hit him, hurling the full weight of his body behind a punch that struck Madden like a hammer-blow in the chest.

Madden staggered, slamming his back against the crumpled frame of the sports car. The branch fell from his hand and Stefan took three quick paces forward, going after him with his right hand cocked.

Stefan's left hand clamped tight around Madden's throat and he squeezed with all his strength. Then he used his right, punching up under the big man's exposed ribs, tearing stomach muscles.

Stefan landed a flurry of blows. Some were too high and with each wayward impact he heard Madden's ribs crack and snap.

Finally Stefan took a step back and Madden slowly sagged face forward. Stefan hit him flush in the mouth with a left hook that snapped his teeth off at the gums and split his top lip wide open.

Stefan reached into his trouser pocket and flicked open his cell phone. He dialed 911.

"There's been a car accident just east of the old Gatfield turnoff," he said, sounding much calmer than he felt. "One man injured. Take your time."

He reached down and grabbed a handful of Madden's hair, then dragged the unconscious man out of the pool of his own bloody vomit.

When Stefan got back into his car, Renee was waiting for him. She smiled – and the sparkle was back in her eye.

Twenty.

Two days later Renee and Stefan drove back along the winding road – heading home from the hospital. The late afternoon had tinted the surrounding woodlands with shades of mauve and orange, and the road was a dappled camouflage of light and shadow.

Tink was waiting for them in the open doorway wearing her blue sundress and when Renee embraced her, the young girl began to cry.

"I'm so glad you are better."

"It's going to take a little while longer," Renee whispered, her voice still a painful rasp, "and I could use a little help around the house for a while if you would be willing."

Tink smiled her delight.

Stefan came from the car carrying an overnight bag on his shoulder. He took Renee gently by the elbow and guided her to the bedroom.

In their absence, Tink had cleaned, replaced the linen in the bedroom, and filled the house with bunches of fresh-cut flowers. She hovered in the hallway until Stefan had Renee comfortably in bed and then she shuffled shyly to the open door. Stefan waved to her and she sat quietly at the end of the bed.

"We'd like you to stay for a while," Stefan said to Tink. "The spare room is yours if you'd like it."

Tink nodded. "Is that alright with you?" she asked Renee.

"It was my idea," Renee said.

"I have contacts," Stefan went on. "I know many Masters who would be excited to have you live with them. If you like, I can make some calls."

Tink nodded – but this time her reaction was guarded and unsure. "I... would like that," she began, "but... but I don't want to end up with another Master like Master Larry. And I'm not even sure what makes a Master good – or bad."

Renee reached over to the bedside table and pulled the white card from underneath her diamond bracelet. "This is a gift," she said, "so you will know what makes a good Master great."

Tink read the card slowly, and *'shimmer's'* words brought a mist of tears to her eyes. "Don't you need this?"

"No," Renee smiled. "I have my Master – and my man. It's everything I ever wanted."

* * *

Bonus Material:

Whenever Hollywood releases a new film it's normal for the stars to do a wide range of interviews. I thought it would be fun to send an interviewer to talk to Stefan and Renee.

This interview took place eight weeks after the story concluded:

Interviewer: Well, what a story! Welcome to both of you. Thanks for giving up your time to be interviewed. Renee, I have to ask you straight away how you're feeling. The end of Her Master's Kiss 2 showed you coming home from hospital. That was a couple of months ago. How are you now?

Renee: Fine. Thanks. The first couple of weeks after the story ended were difficult but once the bruising and swelling subsided, I felt much better. There are no long-term issues. I'm pretty-much back to normal. Psychologically...? Well, I think I'm okay now, although I still get a little crazy whenever Stefan goes into Bishop's Bridge without me.

Interviewer: Did you ever suspect, when the story began, that the ending would be so dramatic – and traumatic?

Renee: No! We had no idea what Vivian Sparx had planned, and so the way the story developed... well we were expecting something very different. We expected the story to show how the relationship between Stefan and I deepened... we just never anticipated that something so dramatic would be the catalyst for the change in our relationship.

Interviewer: Stefan, the conch. What a wonderful idea! How has that beautiful bracelet changed the way you and Renee interact with each other?

Stefan: As I said in the story, the bracelet was a way of me opening up to Renee, and slowly beginning to transform our relationship from a strict Master/submissive relationship to one that was much deeper. Having lived with Renee, and knowing my feelings for her were changing, it was my way of opening the door a little, but still retaining a measure of control.

Interviewer: And now?

Stefan: Well now Renee wears the bracelet all the time. In fact the Master/submissive relationship we once had has pretty-much been abandoned. I don't feel I need to hold on to control anymore. I feel.... I feel like the man I was when my first wife was alive. I'm happy to be in a loving, equal relationship now. In fact the BDSM aspect we structured everything on has essentially become a much lighter, sensual part of the bigger picture.

Renee: I have to say that Stefan has been wonderful. Since the end of our story, we've become much, much closer. Sometimes I make him angry just for fun... and that's when the sparks fly and we revert to our previous roles for an hour or two....

But apart from that I feel like I am Stefan's equal within the relationship, and I really love the fact that he listens to my thoughts and feelings and respects me as a woman.

Interviewer: The real transformation in this story is how you come to realize exactly how you feel about Renee. Would you agree with that Stefan?

Stefan: Yes, I do agree. I think Vivian Sparx has shown how I've opened up to love, and done a pretty good job of it. I wished she'd found a less dramatic way to show that transformation – but I suppose all is well that ends well...

Interviewer: Stefan, the scene when you discover Renee has been beaten and attacked by Larry Madden. Can you talk us through that? Tell us what you were feeling.

Stefan: Sparx described it all quite well. I don't think there's much more I can add.

Interviewer: Really?

Stefan: Look – it was a very difficult moment, and not one I want to re-visit just for an interview. The silver-lining to that scene was that it made me realize just how much I loved Renee. If that's the quote you want, then you can have it. But I don't wish to go over the other emotions of that scene. It was intense, and it was frightening for me. That's all I'm prepared to discuss at this stage.

Interviewer: Okay. Moving on then. The moment when you saw Madden standing in the roadway as you were driving Renee to the hospital. How fierce was the urge for revenge?

Stefan: It was so fierce I honestly considered running the man down and killing him. I did. It was only a fleeting thought – but that's the truth. And when I got out of the car my first instinct was to kill him.

Interviewer: You beat him up pretty badly.

Stefan: Nowhere near as badly as he deserved.

Interviewer: Let me just ask you something that I've been wondering about, Stefan. In the story there is a scene where you and Renee are discussing your past, and you mention a man named Victor. Is this man still... still doing what he does?

Stefan: Trafficking young girls? Training them to be sex slaves for wealthy men? Is that what you mean?

Interviewer: Yes.

Stefan: I honestly don't know. As I said, I was never involved in that dark and dangerous side of the lifestyle. But I can say this: if he is not involved in this disgusting practice, then someone else is.

Hundreds of young girls go missing around this country every year....

Interviewer: That leads me to my next question, and it's for you Renee. I want you to talk about the young girl Tink. What's happened since the end of the story?

Renee: Tink! She's wonderful. You know I really do think Tink's journey was the highlight of this story for me. I know there was a lot of emotion and drama... and a dash of action, but I think Tink's contribution to the storyline, and the way she emerged was just wonderful.

Interviewer: And now?

Renee: She still lives with Stefan and me – for the moment at least. She has been a great help around the home, and she's been a good friend. Stefan has introduced her to a Master he knows who lives an hour away from us, and Tink has been spending some time with him – just getting to know and understand each other. I don't know if they will form a Master/submissive relationship... but at this stage it looks promising. Stefan even offered to dismantle the punishment room downstairs and convert it into a one bedroom flat for her. We'll see.

Interviewer: Stefan? Is that true? Would you really dismantle the punishment room?

Stefan: Yes. I don't feel Renee and I have a need for it anymore. It served its purpose. I think the space could be used for much better things.

Interviewer: Well, as a final question for you both, tell us about what you think the future holds. Renee, have you thought about life ahead for you and Stefan?

Renee: Every day! What girl doesn't dream about her future? If you're asking me whether I dream about marrying this man one day, then of course the answer is yes!

Interviewer: Stefan? This is an exciting possibility. Are the wedding bells ringing in your future?

Stefan: Don't even mention a wedding! The last think we want to do is give Vivien Sparx any more ideas...

Interviewer: Renee? Do you have anything you want to say? Have you spoken to Vivien Sparx? Surely a wedding would be the ultimate fairytale conclusion to your journey with Stefan.

Renee: I do have an exciting secret to share with everyone who has followed our story. I can announce right now that ——

(*interview abruptly terminated at the insistence of Stefan*)

Made in the USA
Lexington, KY
16 March 2013